P9-DCM-654

A Traveling Cat

by GEORGE ELLA LYON

Illustrated by

PAUL BRETT JOHNSON

Orchard Books New York

For Steve, Benn, and Joey
in memory of Comet
—G.E.L.

To Carlie—P.B.J.

Orchard Books, 95 Madison Avenue, New York, NY 10016

Manufactured in the United States of America
Printed by Barton Press, Inc. Bound by Horowitz/Rae
Book design by Mina Greenstein
The text of this book is set in 16 point Veljovic Medium.
The illustrations are colored pencil.

10 9 8 7 6 5 4 3 2 1

Library of Congress Cataloging-in-Publication Data
Lyon, George Ella, date.
A traveling cat / by George Ella Lyon ; illustrated by Paul Brett Johnson.
  p. cm.
Summary: When discovered on the playground in front of the drive-in movie
screen, Boulevard, a stray cat, stays in her new home for a short while before
taking to the road.
ISBN 0-531-30102-8 (trade : alk. paper)—ISBN 0-531-33102-4 (lib. bdg. : alk. paper)
1. Cats—Juvenile fiction. [1. Cats—fiction.] I. Johnson, Paul Brett, ill. II. Title.
PZ10.3.L9875Tr   1998 [E]—dc21   98-13796

*B*oulevard was a traveling cat.
We named her after the road.

She didn't come from the pet store.
She didn't come from a friend.
I found her at the drive-in movie
on the playground in front of the screen.

The movie started
and Bouvie followed me
all the way to the car.
When Dad opened the door,
she jumped in.
"Ruth's found a hitchhiker!" he said,
picking Bouvie up.
"Now whose little cat could you be?"

Dad asked the man at the concession stand.
My brother, Ted, asked the family who lives in the screen.
Mom and I asked folks in the cars around us.
No one was missing a cat.
"Guess she's ours," I said.

Bouvie had a night-colored coat
splattered with gold, like stars.
She *did* swing from the curtains,
but even Mom said she was graceful.
And she loved to sit on the dryer,
watching squirrels out the window like TV.

Come fall, she had kittens
somewhere in the woods.
For a week she kept them hidden.

Then came a big storm.
Bouvie caterwauled at the door—
we heard her above the thunder.
She carried in Cupid, curled like a bug,
and dropped him at our feet.

Four more trips she made
into the stormy woods
to bring Peaches,
        Lightning,
            Midnight,
                and Bruce.

When the kittens were ready to play outside,
Bouvie caught a bird to show them.
They sat in front of her like kids at school
while she meowed, the bird at her feet.
"She's teaching them how to hunt," Mom said.
They ate their lesson up.

Then Roscoe, Papa Bill's beagle,
followed his nose down the street.
Like a shooting star, Boulevard
streaked to Roscoe's back.
Claws dug in, she hung on
while he did his best to run.
Ted said he'd never seen a cat
catch a ride on a dog.

By Christmas we had given away
all the kittens but Bruce.
He spent the winter with Boulevard,
sleeping by the fireplace,
dancing in the snow.

Spring came: flood time.
Animals knew it first.
They were gone before the water hit the bridge:
the Cains' dog, Shirley,
the Macs' dog, Toy,
Boulevard, even Roscoe.
Everybody but Bruce.
They all went to high ground
somewhere in the hills.
Only Toy came back.

All summer I've looked for my cat,
especially at the drive-in.
Once I took Bruce with me,
but he's not like his mama—
he hid under the seat.

Dad says Boulevard stayed a long time
for such a traveling cat.
Maybe, but not long enough.
Mom says probably Boulevard
hiked on over to Virginia
and slipped out of the woods
into another family's life.
If she did, I'd like to tell them,
"Don't expect to keep her.
She's a traveling cat.

Her home is the road."